One Smiling Grandma

A CARIBBEAN COUNTING BOOK

For my beloved Maharaj Charan Singh ji
A.M.L.

For Trevor with love
L.R.

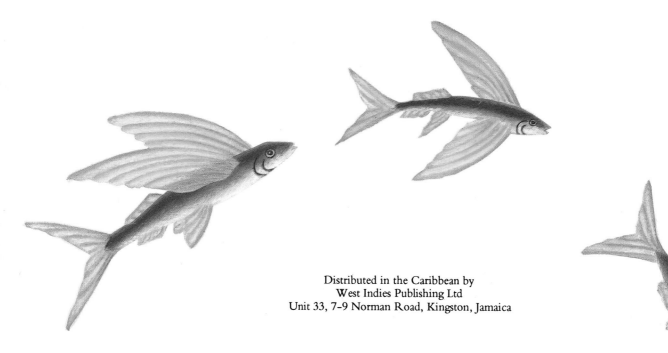

Distributed in the Caribbean by
West Indies Publishing Ltd
Unit 33, 7-9 Norman Road, Kingston, Jamaica

First published in Great Britain 1992
by William Heinemann Limited
an imprint of Reed Consumer Books Ltd
Michelin House, 81 Fulham Road, London SW3 6RB
and Auckland, Melbourne, Singapore and Toronto

Reprinted 1993

ISBN 0 434 94209 X
Produced by Mandarin Offset
Printed and bound in Hong Kong

One Smiling Grandma

A CARIBBEAN COUNTING BOOK

ANN MARIE LINDEN

Illustrated by

LYNNE RUSSELL

HEINEMANN · LONDON

One smiling grandma in a rocking chair,

Two yellow bows tied on braided hair.

Three hummingbirds sipping nectar sweet,

Four steel drums tapping out the beat.

Five flying fish gliding through the air,

Six market ladies selling their wares.

Seven conch shells I find on the beach,

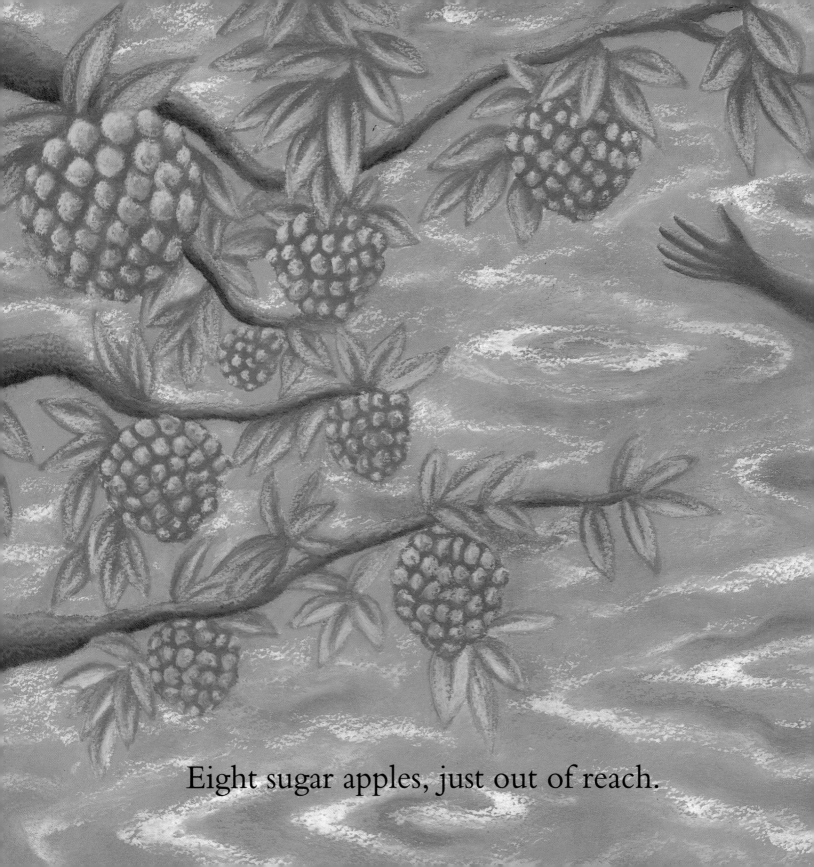

Eight sugar apples, just out of reach.

Nine hairy coconuts, hard and round,

Ten sleepy mongoose,

Hush!
Not a sound.